river man

by don hurd

published by deep throat giraffe

If he tells me all he knows
About the way his river flows
I don't suppose
It's meant for me

Nick Drake

For Jim Magill

1

I kept the key in my pocket, the key
Dolores had given me the last time I saw
her. I never wanted to enter through that
door again, but knowing it was not
locked to me, that if I ever I chose to
enter I had the means to do so, removed
any desire to be where I had once longed
to be with every fiber of my being. I was
free, as free as anyone can be and still
walk under the bulbous sun or lie
beneath the cool net of stars. The
nightingales sang in the cool, growing
light of dawn, and I sang in my heart.
Dolores was gone, and in her leaving had
set me free.

2

And so it was this morning I rose to the smell of honeysuckle drifting through my open window. I kicked off the covers in the night as I did every night. I lay there naked in the cool air, conscious of the tightness of my own skin. All those days spent lying under the sun on the leatherette lounger, smoking cigarettes, reading Ionesco and Tzara, feeling my desire to be anything, anyone, anywhere else, shrivel within in me like a raisin. Even my desire for...

3

Dolores the huntress, Dolores the muse, Dolores the Madonna, the bright-haired Dolores who sang nonsense songs into my ears, who coaxed the wax from my ears as easily as she coaxed the phrases she required from my lips, signifying my submission to her bountiful presence, Dolores the instigator, Dolores the enticer, reveling in the convulsive act of love, Dolores the first and last lover of my life, Dolores the dead and buried...

4

I drew on the same pair of soiled slacks and loose-fitting smock that always made me feel like Picasso, put sandals on my unwashed feet. There would be cold coffee from last night and a record on the turntable. I drank the coffee from a glass and put the needle on the record. It was the same record I'd been listening to for the past three weeks, the 7th symphony by Beethoven. I listened only to the first movement, picking up the needle just before the second movement began and starting it over again and again. Long intervals of time passed in this way, time that seemed like the record to start over again and again, the same music, another glass of coffee, and the same two books, read and reread. Dolores hated Beethoven.

5

She would suck on her teeth and roll her
eyes, and once began to jitterbug across
the floor, nude, slapping her hands on
her thighs, humming then nasally
warbling snatches from show tunes until
I turned off the record. Intolerant
Dolores, brutally fascist in her tastes, her
demand for complete attention.

6

I drink the cold coffee and listen to Beethoven, stare at the mists, the transfiguration of faces. I could no longer hear the shadows, the shadows that once raised a din in my mind, like a brass orchestra thundering the end of a film in which the final moments are a colossal rebuke of everything we thought mattered, leaving us to stare at the blank screen as our final end, the summation of negation. I could no longer hear the shadows barking at me like a pack of pariahs. I could no longer hear the shadows.

7

There is a tension that comes from the absence of strife, as if sensing the vacuum we have to fill it. It can lead to random acts of destructiveness, like the day I broke the vase, or the time I set fire to all my bed sheets. The mice in my brain gnaw at silence. The horses in my veins tug at the reins. It begins and ends with silence. Dolores biting her lower lip, running her hands across her smooth belly, spreading her legs until I could see her sex, saying nothing, inviting destruction. I didn't kill her. I didn't kill her. I didn't kill her. I only killed her after she was already dead, when it was necessary to fill that most terrible silence. I killed her with Beethoven.

8

The nightingales warble and thrum. The shadows are tuneless. I see only the faces I love in the quickly dispersing mists. I never see Dolores, but she is there, waiting in the shadows.

9

I lift the needle and start the first movement again. Time repeats itself. Again. I am only alone when I am happy. In the past, when I was torn apart with the din of shadows, the faces that thronged outside my colorless windows were a torment. I do not see them now.

10

In a few hours the woman who cooks will come. I have forgotten her name. I don't think I ever knew it. She could be anyone. Yes, even Dolores. She could be Dolores. She has fat ankles and short nubs for fingers. She cooks and I eat what she cooks. If she wanted to, she could poison me. Why would she want to poison me? But she could if she wanted to. I do not think she wants to.

11

Start the record again.

Last night I was visited by the laughing ghosts. It started in a bowl of fruit that had soured, blackened bananas, shriveled, pocked apples splotched with brown. Everything starts somewhere. The sound of their laughter, the ghosts, was like hundreds of small fish flopping on hot stones. I put on Beethoven and turned it up loud. The laughter increased. In the cacophony I clearly heard the hard, guttural laugh of Dolores, laughter that rose, when she was alive, from deep within her bowels and shook her whole body. Laughter that ran down the long sluice of derision until it gushed forth like a geyser. Laughter entirely without joy for when Dolores was happy she never laughed.

13

Dolores in white boots and black velvet gloves, her lips drawn back, her teeth bare, her shoulders shaking mirthlessly as I stand accusingly holding a letter, the letter, my face red with rage, Dolores gathering from a dark, secret organ the laugh that would burst from her reddened lips at the very moment the groan of despair escaped from mine before I turned and ran from the apartment into the callous streets of that far away city under the mocking gaze of gargoyles perched stonily astride colossal buildings that towered and swayed as I ran to the river still hearing the sound of her laughter in my ears until I reached the embankment and gazed down into the swiftly moving water, black as velvet, swirling with brine, a vortex of darkness that ended, far distant, in the unimaginable depths of the ocean. And all around me the vast hosts of the defeated gathered and their laughter joined with hers in an unharmonious chorus.

15

I took the bowl of fruit outside and buried it, turning over spadefulls of night black earth. When I was done, I leaned on the shovel and gazed up at the stars. A thousand black umbrellas opened and closed in my mind. I could hear the 7th from inside the house. The humid night air was thick with the smell of honeysuckle. The ghosts were silent. My bare feet reached down into the cool earth, feeling the pulsation of blind creatures toiling beneath the packed soil, the tumult of roots writhing against softening resistance, exploring like elongated tongues, tumescent and terrifying, while I stood, rooted as a headstone, straining to regain the muscled memory of movement, escape, freedom. The second movement began, the insistent pathos of strings bent to one purpose, while my mouth opened and soundlessly I mouthed her name, the name of my destructress, my angelic one, my demon.

Gazing upward I watched in horror as a black-velveted glove plucked from the sky one by one the stars.

17

The ambassador arrived this morning and stood outside my window eating grapes out of his hat. I waved to him from the wash basin and, throwing a towel around my neck for my hair was wet went out to the patio to greet him.

"There are nine cats in your yard," he informed me, and held up nine chubby fingers sticky with grape juice.

"They don't belong to me," I replied.

"My father says you cannot own cats."

"Your father is a wise man."

The ambassador shrugged. "He doesn't have any money."

I reached into his hat and extracted a handful of grapes. They were sweet and cool.

18

"I am going to the bridge today," he informed me. "There is going to be the bathing with the tourists. The women bathe, too, just like the men."

I nodded. The ambassador was perhaps ten years old. I called him the ambassador because he was the first person from the village to come to my house a few days after my arrival. He had a large head, bushy black hair, and oval eyes the color of burnt milk.

"What did you bury over there?" he asked.

"Some fruit that had gone bad."

He nodded as if this was perfectly understandable.

19

"I'm going now," he said, stuffing the last of grapes into his mouth and putting his cap back on his head.

"I will name a cloud after you," I told him as he was about to jump over the low wall. He looked up at the sky.

"Which one?"

I pointed. "That fat one with the long nose."

He jumped onto the wall and over it. I saw his head bobbing away beneath the cloud that bore his name, a name I had never learned.

It was Dolores who first named the clouds. Sometimes she would look up at the sky and exclaim, "Look! It's Michael. He's come back!"

No, it wasn't Dolores. Dolores never named anything, not even the cats.

I saw Michael the day she died. He rained.

20

A river of sweat runs down my right temple. I used to enjoy sweating when I was a boy, savoring the taste of my own perspiration. It is hotter here than any place I have ever lived. Even the insects cannot manage to rise more than a few inches above the ground. There is a fly on my ankle. He is drinking my sweat perhaps. I should go down to the river like the tourists. I have seen their footprints in the muddy bank, watched the ambassador fill with his urine one enormous cavity left by a giant of a tourist. He performed this trick in absolute seriousness.

21

I scratch my armpit and stare at the distant hills radiant in the afternoon sun. The bees drone near the empty clay pots beside the house. Gazing over the open mouths of these pots I see dark, half-moon smiles.

Start the record again.

23

The river terrifies me. I cannot dislodge the illusion from my mind that the river is wider than the banks that contain it, that it runs beneath the pocked and footprinted mud, beneath the loose shale, the polished stones, the sand and tufts of weeds, extending for hundreds of yards outward and unseen, beneath the surface. I know that if I stand there too long the river will suck me down, through the choking mud, into the cold, deep heart of the world.

24

I taste my own sweat. The clay pots are smiling their dark, earthen smiles. I hear the woman moving about the house. It will be time for lunch soon and I'll eat whatever she gives me. In the three months since I arrived, I have never once refused a meal. I'm gaining weight, actually. Like all foreign cooks, she believes in fattening her employer. I don't mind. I could be a fat old man someday, but that won't happen now.

25

The angled light of evening strikes the ceramic head of a fawn. I am sitting on the floor with a basket of figs. The fawn is staring at me with luminous, serious eyes. Somewhere a clock must be ticking. I have reached a place inside myself where all the clocks are ticking. In the dark heart of the forest, a fawn is trembling. I eat the flesh of the figs, sitting cross-legged on the floor. Once, I took the hand of a girl and led her into a haystacked barn. It was night and we could hear the mice gnawing in the darkness beyond the lamp. I stood over her as she stretched on her back, inviting, her hair tangled with hay. Somewhere in the distance a peacock was crying. I stretched out on top of her and she gasped with my weight. I knew nothing about the sexual act. She looked up at me like a wounded fawn. All that night, as I lay in bed afterwards, I could hear my uncle's clock ticking, I could hear the mice gnawing. I turned over in my sleep to dream of a fawn running through the forest and first I was the fawn and then I was the hunter and finally I became the forest. I take another fig from the basket, spread it open with my thumbs, and devour the sweet flesh within. The room is getting darker and soon the ceramic fawn is lost in another forest. I stretch out on my back and whisper her name... no, it was not Dolores.

27

I tried to cross the river today. The ambassador went with me.

This was to be my first trip across the river since my arrival, and one that the ambassador had been trying to organize for weeks. The idea was to visit another village a few miles distant where, he claimed, there was a shop that sold American whiskey. I've never been a heavy drinker, but I had grown tired of drinking cold coffee.

It had not escaped my notice that the river itself was a powerful symbol. Once, I am told, it rose beyond its grassy banks and swallowed half the village. That was more than half a century ago. The bridge, too, was a potent metaphor, bridging the gap between the world I left behind and my current existence. Yet I knew one day I would cross it, one day I would return to the world I abandoned. So today's trip was an experiment. I felt ready.

The ambassador was in high spirits. His father, who ran a small shop in the village, had sold several expensive items to a tourist from Belgium.

"They pay so much money," said the ambassador, rubbing his fingers together in a manner he had no doubt picked up from his father. "And for nothing. My father says we could sell them petrified dog shit."

I was hardly listening because we were approaching the bridge. The ambassador was kicking at the loose stone making a spray of pebbles with every step. I slowed down and he got ahead of me, still jabbering away about the stupidity of tourists.

29

I was looking across at the far bank. An old tire was lying on its side just above the water line. It had been washed down river in the last deluge perhaps. Weeds sprouted from the hollow. It might have been the eye-socket of some slain beast, or even the anus.

"Come on," said the ambassador, who had finally noticed my lagging. He squatted on the pavement and picked at a scab on his kneecap.

I stepped onto the bridge, my right hand on the concrete rail. I moved forward slowly. Even though I tried not to think about it, I knew the eye on the embankment was watching me, or, to put it even more absurdly, I felt myself under the watchful gaze of that anus. With every step I took the obscene artifact swam before my eyes as if it was once more a captive of the savage river. Reluctantly, I began to assemble this creature in my thoughts, its enormous haunches, the matted fur on its belly, the pitifully thin legs. I heard its desolate cry as it wandered up and down some father bank, desperately seeking its lower orifice. I wanted to comfort it, to reach out and caress its hairy snout!

"Aren't you coming?" said the ambassador impatiently.

I turned on my heel and left, but all the way home I was haunted by my inability to console the beast in my imagination.

31

Last night I dreamed of Robert Mitchum. He was dressed in a long raincoat, sitting on a bench in a train station. As he waited, he worked on a crossword puzzle in a newspaper. He used an enormous pencil. It was a very difficult puzzle because the paper was written in several languages. His face was very serious. Finally the train arrived. Mitchum folded the paper and put it in his pocket. The doors of the train opened and these beautiful women got off and they were all the same. They were all my darling Dolores.

It's been raining for four days. The yard around the house has turned into a lake. Dozens of snails have crawled up the walls. Even from this distance, I can hear the river's raging current. The ambassador turned up today, dressed in a makeshift raincoat made of plastic bags and an enormous pair of rubber boots. He said the river is already almost to the bottom of the bridge. All sorts of flotsam have washed downstream: a birdcage, a guitar, a crate filled with cantaloupes, and, strangest of all, an ornate mirror with cherubs carved into the frame.

"Maybe it will wash away the whole village this time," he said. The prospect did not seem to worry him.

He gave me three cantaloupes and left.

33

At sunset the rapid clouds gave me the sense of the planet spinning in almost the same way that standing on the deck of a ship makes one feel that nothing is really moving. I stretched out my legs and let my arms fall limply to the ground. Closing my eyes, I was lifted up among the clouds like a balloon tethered to the little house below me, to my own inert body. Briefly, I imagined myself a kite. I pulled the string and watched as I performed advanced aerial acrobatics. Running across a fresh green field, I held tightly to the string as I watched my kite-self being dragged across the sky and then at the same time looked down from my heavenly position to see myself running across the field. Then, from nearby copse, Dolores emerged and ran toward me, her white legs kicking up the hem of a sky-blue dress. In her hand she held a pair of shining scissors.

Will I ever be free? Will she ever cut the tether?

34

I opened my eyes to see that the clouds were gone and the sky had turned to night. Overhead, a field of faintly throbbing stars peppered the blackness like lost periods in search of unfinished sentences.

35

This morning I found in my coffee cup the corpse of a moth. I stared at it for several moments, then fished it out and laid it across a scrap of newspaper, spreading its wings and patting them dry. In the afternoon, I carefully placed the dead moth between the pages of a collection of Mallarme's poetry Dolores gave me for my birthday even though she knew I could not read French. One poem still bears the pencil marking of my laborious attempt to translate a poem using a French-English dictionary. As I closed the book, I was assaulted by the remembered aroma of baking bread because at the time Dolores and I lived above a bakery. The fat little baker's wife had the smallest hands I have ever seen that did not belong to a child.

When we moved out of the apartment, I bowed and kissed her knuckles and they tasted like cinnamon.

Dolores had a large mole on her right thigh. She never wore short skirts because the mole embarrassed her. I loved it. Often, when we made love, I would run my fingers across it. Though this bothered her at first, in time she permitted it and would even joke about my obsession. "You only love me for my little mole," she scoffed. Well, it was certainly not little, but I wasn't about to quibble. I explored her body like Magellan. I knew every little islet, every continent, and all the deep rivers that ran just below the surface waiting for a caress to send her into shivers of sensual pleasure. I nestled for hours between her breasts, spent an eternity adoring the rosy mounds of her buttocks. Yet, for all the pleasures this landscape offered me, none was as

37

fascinating to me as that mole. And now
it is gone, forever, unless, in some
unimaginable realm, her flesh should
once again take form, and I, rescued
from the oblivion of life itself, should
find myself worshipping at that erotic
altar and reach down to find the little
brown nub of happiness.

38

I woke up this morning to find Dolores in bed beside me.

"You're dead," I told her.

"I came back."

"It doesn't work like that."

"Sometimes it does."

I put my hand under the covers and felt her body; it was warm and soft.

"I killed you myself."

"You wish!" She got out of bed and pulled on her dress. "I think it's time we were going."

"I like it here."

"Mmm. All day listening to your Beethoven, I imagine. Feeling sorry for yourself? That's all over now."

"Where will we go?"

"Wherever we want to." She took a pair of scissors out of her pocket and very swiftly cut a lock of her hair and brushed it against my lips. "There's so much to tell you."

I put my hand on her thigh, searching with my fingers.

38

"Where is it?" I said.

"The little mole?" she said, smiling. "I had it removed. It was cancerous."

I nodded. "Yes, I remember now."

She got up and took me by the hand. "Time to go."

I dressed while she waited. Then I looked around the room. "Can I bring something?"

"Of course."

I went into the outer room and she followed me. I picked up the volume of Mallarme and she laughed. "Oh, no! You'll never get it translated properly!"

"I know, but it means something to me." I looked inside. "That's odd."

"What?"

"I put something inside this book, but it's gone now."

She brushed her hand through her hair and a white moth flew out.

39

It was all very clear to me then. I walked over to the record player as she rolled her eyes. "Please, not that!" she laughed.

I started the record again and we left.

40

I drifted down the river on a makeshift raft constructed from the flotsam of my life: my aunt's wardrobe, an old bookcase, my grandfather's spinning globe, a leather-bound set of Dickens. The face of the river was as smooth as glass and I watched the reflection of clouds pass beneath me as I floated along. The entire village turned out to watch my departure. Among them I saw the faces of many people I knew. I called to them but they did not answer. They watched solemnly as I drifted past.

The Ambassador was standing on the bridge. He waved to me and I waved back. Gradually the banks grew wider until they disappeared from view.

Finally I reached the open sea. I placed my hand upon the spinning globe and stared out across the untroubled blue waters...

Start the record again.

index

a

7th 4,15
a 2,4,6,7,12,
13, 15-20,24 -
29,31 -36
abandoned
27
about 15,19,
24, 28,29,36
above 20,29,
35
absence 7
absolute 20
absurdly 29
accusingly 13
acrobatics 33
across 5,7,27,
29,33,35, 36
act 3,26
acts 7
actually 24

adoring 36
advanced 33
aerial 33
after 7,18,19
afternoon 21,
35
afterwards 26
Again 9
again 1,4,9,
11, 22,37,40
against 15,38
ago 27
ahead 28
air 2,15
alive 12
All 2,26,32,38
all 7,14,24,25,
30,31,32,26,
38,40
almost 32,33

aroma 35
around 14,17,
32,39
arrival 18,27
arrived 17,24,
31
artifact 29
As 31,35
as 1-3,6,7,13,
15,16,18,19,2
5,26,29,30,33,
36,37,40
asked 18
assaulted 35
assemble 29
astride 13
At 6,7,13,15,
19,21,25,26,
28,29,33,35,3
6,37

attempt 35
attention 5
away 13,19,
28,32

b

behind 27
being 1,33
Belgium 28
believes 24
belly 7,30
belong 17,35
below 33,36
bench 31
beneath 1,15,
19,23
bent 16
beside 21,38
between 27,
35,36
beyond 25,27
birdcage 32
birthday 35
biting 7
black 13,15,
16,18

blackened 12
blackness 34
blank 6
blind 15
blue 33
bobbing 19
body 12,33,
36,38
book 35,39
books 4
boots 13
boots 32
bore 19
bothered 36
bottom 32
bountiful 3
bowed 35
bowels 12
bowl 12,15
boy 20

brain 7
brass 6
bread 35
breasts 36
bridge 18,27,
28,29,32
bridging 27
Briefly 33
bright 3
brine 13
bring 39
broke 7
brown 12,37
brushed 38,
39
brutally 5
buildings 13
bulbous 1
buried 3,15
burnt 18

burst 13
bury 18
bushy 18
But 10
but 1,8,24,27,
30,36,39
buttocks 36
by 4,12,16,20,
30,35,39

C

cacophony 12
called 18
callous 13
came 38
can 1,7,32,39
cancerous 39
cannot 17,20, 23
cantaloupes 32
cap 19
captive 29
carefully 35
caress 30,36
carved 32
cats 17,19
cavity 20
century 27
ceramic 25,26
certainly 36

cherubs 32
child 35
choking 23
chorus 14
chose 1
chubby 17
cigarettes 2
cinnamon 35
city 13
claimed 27
clay 21,24
clear 40
clearly 12
clock 25,26
clocks 25
closed 15,35
Closing 33
cloud 19
clouds 19,33, 34

cut 33,38

d

dark 13
dark 21,24,25
darker 26
darkness
13,25
darling 31
dawn 1
day 7,19,27,
38
days 2,1,18,
32
dead 3,7,35,
38
deck 33
deep 12,23,36
defeated 14
deluge 29
demand 5
demon 16
depths 14

derision 12
desire 1,2
desolate 30
despair 13
desperately
30
destruction 7
destructivene
ss 7
destructress
16
devour 26
dictionary 35
did 2,18,32,
35
didn't 7
died 19
difficult 31
din 6,9
dislodge 23

dispersing 8
distance 25, 32
distant 14,21, 27
do 1,9,10
does 38
doesn't 17,38
dog 18
Dolores 1,3, 4,5,7,8,10,12, 13,19,26,31, 33,35,36,38
don't 10,17, 24
done 15
door 1
doors 31
doubt 28

down 12,13, 15,20,23,28, 29,30,33,37
downstream 32
Dozens 32
dragged 33
drank 4
drawn 13
dream 26
dreamed 31
dress 33,38
dressed 31, 32,39
drew 4
drifting 2
drink 6
drinker 27
drinking 20, 27

e

ears 3,13
earth 15
earthen 24
easily 3
eat 10,24,25
eating 17
elongated 15
else 2
embankment 13,29,36
emerged 33
employer 24
empty 21
end 6
ended 14
ends 7
English 35
enjoy 20
enormous 20, 29,31,32

enter 1
enticer 3
entirely 12
erotic 37
escape 15
escaped 13,27
eternity 36
Even 2,20,29, 32
even 10,19,29, 35,36
evening 25
ever 1,10,20, 33,35
every 1,2,28, 29,36
Everything 12
everything 6

face 13,31
faces 6,8,9
faintly 34
fall 33
far 13,14,29
fascinating 37
fascist 5
fat 10,19,24,
35
father 17
father 28,30
fattening 24
fawn 25,26
feel 4,33
feeling 2,15
Feeling 38
feet 4,15
felt 27,29,38
few 10,18,20,
27

fiber 1
field 33,34
fig 26
figs 25
fill 7,20
filled 32
film 6
final 6
Finally 31
finally 26,29
find 37,38
fingers 10,17,
28,36,38
fire 7
first 3,4,9,18,
19,26,27,36
fish 12
fished 35
fitting 4
flesh 25,26,37

flew 39
floor 5,25
flopping 12
flotsam 32
fly 20
folded 31
followed 39
footprinted 23
footprints 20
for 2,4,5,10, 12,17,23,24,2 7,28,32,35,36, 38
foreign 24,31
forest 25,26
forever 37
forgotten 10
form 37
forth 12

forward 29
found 35
four 32
frame 32
free 1,33
freedom 15
French 35
fresh 33
from 3,4,5,7, 12,13,15,16, 17,18,23,26, 28,29,32,33, 37
fruit 12,15,18
fur 30

g

gaining 24
gap 27
gargoyles 13
gasped 25
gathered 14
gathering 13
gave 21,32, 33,35
gaze 13,29
gazed 13,15
Gazing 16,21
get 39
getting 26
geyser 12
ghosts 12,15
giant 20
girl 25
given 1
gives 24
glass 4

glove 16
gloves 13
gnaw 7
gnawing 25, 26
go 20,38,39
going 18,19, 38
gone 1,18,34, 37,39
got 28,31,38, 39
grape 17
grapes 17,19
grassy 27
green 33
greet 17
groan 13
ground 20,33
growing 1

grown 27
guitar 32
gushed 12
guttural 12

h

had 1,12,18,
19,27,28,29,
34,35,36,39
hair 17,18,25,
38,39
haired 3
hairy 30
half 27
halfmoon 21
hand 25,29,
33,38,39
handful 17
hands 5,7,25
happen 24
happiness 37
happy 9,12
hard 12
hardly 28
has 10,32
hat 17

hated 4
haunches 30
haunted 30
have 7,10,17,
20,24,25,29,3
2,35
hay 25
haystacked 25
He 17,18,19,
20,29,31,32
he 17,18,19,
27, 28,31,32
head 18,19,25
headstone 15
hear 6,15,24,
25,26,32
heard 12,30
hearing 13
heart 1,23,25
heavenly 33

heavy 27
heel 30
held 17,33
hem 33
her 1,3,5,7,
10,12,13,16,
24-26,33,35-
40
here 20,38
hers 14
high 28
hills 21
him 17,18,19,
32
His 28,31
his 17,19,20,
28, 29
holding 13
hollow 29
home 30

honeysuckle
2,15
horror 16
horses 7
hosts 14
hot 12
hotter 20
hours 10,36
house 15,18,
21,24,31,33
humid 15
humming 5
hundreds 12,
23
hunter 26
huntress 3

i

24,25,27,29,
31,32,38-40
it 1,2,4,7,10,
12,15,19,23,
26,27,29,30-
32,35-39
items 28
its 27,29,30,
35
itself 9,27,37
I've 27

jabbering 28
jitterbug 5
joined 14
joke 36
joy 12
juice 17
jump 19
jumped 19
just 4,18,29,
36

k

kept 1
key 1
kicked 2
kicking 28,33
kill 7
killed 7,38
kissed 35
kite 33
kiteself 33
kneecap 29
knew 10,25,
27, 29,35,36
know 23,39
knowing 1
knuckles 35

1

laborious 35
lagging 29
laid 35
lake 32
lamp 25
landscape 36
languages 31
large 18,36
last 1,3,4
Last 12,31
last 1,3,4,19,
29
laugh 12,13
laughed 12,
39,40
laughing 12
Laughter 12
laughter 12,
13,14
lay 2,26

lead 7
leaned 15
learned 19
leatherette 2
leaving 1,6
led 25
left 20,27,30,
32,40
legged 25
legs 7,30,33
let 33
letter 13
lie 1
life 3,37
lift 9
lifted 33
light 1,25
Like 24
like 2,4,6,7,
12,

15,18,20,26,3
3,34,35,36,38
limply 33
line 29
lip 7
lips 3,13,38
listen 6
listened 4
listening 4,28,
38
little 33,35,
36, 37,39
lived 20,35
lock 38
locked 1
Long 4
long 12,19,
23,31
longed 1
longer 6

Look 19
look 19
looked 19,26,
33,39
looking 29
loose 4,23,28
lost 26,34
loud 12
lounger 2
love 3,8,36
loved 36
lover 3
low 19
lower 7,30
luminous 25
lunch 24
lying 2,29

m

n

naked 2
name 10,16,
19,26
named 18
nasally 5
near 21
nearby 33
necessary 7
neck 17
needle 4,9
negation 6
nestled 36
net 1
never 1,8,12,
19,24,27,36,3
9
newspaper
31,35
night 2,4

night 2,4,12,
15,25,26,31,
34
nightingales
1,8
nine 17
No 19
no 6,26,28
nodded 18,39
none 36
nonsense 3
nose 19
Not 39
not 1,9,10,19,
26,27,29,32,
35,36,40
nothing 7,25,
28,33
notice 27
noticed 29

now 9,19,24,
37,38,39
nub 37
nubs 10
nude 5

O

oblivion 37
obscene 29
obsession 36
ocean 14
odd 39
of 1-4,6,7,9,
12-21,23,25-
29,31-39
off 2,5,31
offered 36
Often 36
old 18,24,29
on 2,4,5,12,
15,19,20,25,
26,29,30,31,
33,36,38
Once 25,27
once 1,5,6,24,
29,27
One 35

one 16,19,20,
27,33
only 4,7,8,9,
36
onto 19,29
open 2,21,26
opened 15,
16,31,34
or 1,7,29
oranges 12
orchestra 6
organ 13
organize 27
orifice 30
ornate 32
our 6
out 17,25,26,
30
out 33,35,38,
39

outer 39
outside 9,15,
17
outward 23
oval 18
over 4,15,18,
19,21,25,26,3
8,40
Overhead 34
own 2,17,20,
24,33

p

pack 6
packed 15
pages 35
pair 4,32,33, 38
paper 31
pariahs 6
passed 4
past 4,9
pathos 16
patio 17
patting 35
pavement 29
pay 28
peacock 25
pebbles 28
pencil 31,35
peppered 34
perched 13
perfectly 18

performed 20,33
perhaps 18, 20,29
periods 34
permitted 36
person 18
perspiration 20
petrified 28
phrases 3
Picasso 4
picked 28,29, 39
picking 4
pitifully 30
place 20,25
placed 35
planet 33
plastic 32

q

quibble 36
quickly 8

r

radiant 21
rage 13
raging 32
rail 29
raincoat 31,
32
rained 19
raining 32
raised 6
raisin 2
ran 12,13,28,
33,36
random 7
rapid 33
reach 30,37
reached 13,
15,17,25
read 4,35
reading 2
ready 27

really 33
realm 37
rebuke 6
record 4,5,11,
22,40
red 13
reddened 13
refused 24
regain 15
reins 7
Reluctantly
29
remember 39
remembered
35
removed 1,39
repeats 9
replied 17
required 3
reread 4

rescued 37
resistance 15
return 27
reveling 3
right 20,29,36
rise 20
river 13,20,
23, 27,29,32
rivers 36
Robert 31
roll 5
rolled 40
room 26,39
rooted 15
roots 15
rose 2,12,27
rosy 36
rubber 32
rubbing 28
run 36

Running 33
running 7,26,
33
runs 20,23

S

said 19,28,29,
30,32,39
same 4,31,33
sand 23
sandals 4
sang 1,3
savage 29
savoring 20
saw 1,19
saying 7
says 17,28
scab 29
scissors 33,38
scoffed 36
scrap 35
scratch 21
screen 6
search 34
searching 38
second 4,15

secret 13
see 7,8,9,21,
33,34
seeking 30
seem 32
seemed 4
seen 20,35
sell 28
send 36
sense 33
sensing 7
sensual 36
sentences 34
serious 25,31
seriousness
20
set 1,7
several 28,31,
35
sex 7

sexual 25
shadows 6,8, 9
shaking 13
shale 23
She 5,10,26, 36, 38,39
she 3,7,8,10, 12,19,24,25, 33,35,36,39, 40
sheets 7
shining 33
ship 33
shit 28
shivers 36
shook 12
shop 27,28
short 10,36
should 20,37

shoulders 13
shovel 15
show 5
shrivel 2,12
shrugged 17
side 29
signifying 3
silence 7
silent 15
since 24,27
sitting 25,31
skin 2
skirts 36
sky 16,19,33, 34
slacks 4
slain 29
slapping 5
sleep 26
slowed 28

slowly 29

sluice 12

small 12,28

smallest 35

smell 2,15

smiles 21,24

smiling 24,39

smock 4

smoking 2

smooth 7

snails 32

snatches 5

snout 30

So 27

so 1,2,28,38

soft 38

softening 15

soil 15

soiled 4

sold 27,28

Some 18

some 29,30, 37

someday 24

something 39

Sometimes 19,38

Somewhere 25

somewhere 12

songs 3

soon 24,26

sorry 38

sorts 32

sound 12,13

soundlessly 16

soured 12

spadefulls 15

spent 2,36

spinning 33

spirits 28

splotched 12

spray 28

spread 26

spreading 7, 35

sprouted 29

squatted 29

stand 13,23

standing 33

stare 6

stared 35

staring 25

stars 1,15,16, 34

Start 11,22

start 4,9

started 12,40

starting 4

starts 12

station 31

step 28,29

stepped 29

sticky 17

still 1,13,28, 35

stone 28

stones 12,23

stonily 13

stood 15,18, 25

straining 15

strangest 32

streets 13

stretch 26

stretched 25, 33

strife 7

strikes 25

string 33

strings 16

stuffing 19

stupidity 28

submission 3

suck 5,23

summation 6

sun 1,2,21

sunset 33

surface 23,36

swallowed 28

swam 29

swayed 13

sweat 20,24

sweating 20

sweet 17,26

swiftly 13,38

swirling 13

symbol 27

symphony 4

t

take 26,37
tangled 25
taste 20,24
tasted 35
tastes 5
teeth 5,13
tell 38
temple 20
ten 18
tension 7
terrible 7
terrifies 23
terrifying 15
tether 33
tethered 33
than 20,23,27
That 19,27,
38,39
that 1,4,6,7,9,
12-14,18,19,

23, 24,26,27,
29,33-40
The 1,7,8,12,
15,17,18,21,
23-28,31,32,
35,39
the 1-40
their 12,14,
20,24
them 9,28,35
Then 33,39
then 5,26,33,
35,40
There 4,7,17,
18,20,38
there 2,8,18,
23,27
these 21,31
They 17,28,
31,35

u

V

waited 31,39

waiting 8,36

walk 1

walked 40

wall 19

walls 32

wandered 30

want 10,38

wanted 1,10,
30

wants 10

warble 8

warbling 5

warm 38

was 1,2,4,7,9,
12,15,17,18-
20,25-31,33,
35, 36,38-40

wash 17,32

washed 29,32

wasn't 19,36

watched 16,
20,33

watchful 29

watching 29

water 13,29

waved 17

wax 3

way 4,30,33

we 6,7,25,28,
35,26,38,40

Weeds 29

weeds 23

weeks 4,27

weight 24,25

Well 36

went 17,27,29

were 9,15,17,
28,31,34,38

wet 17

women 18,31
won't 24
wore 36
work 38
worked 31
world 23,27
worry 32
worshipping
37
would 4,5,10,
13,19,27,36
wounded 26
writhing 15
written 31

X

y

yard 17,32
yards 23
years 18
Yes 10,39
Yet 27,36
You 36,38,39
you 17,18,19,
30,38
Your 17
your 17,38
yourself 38

Z

www.ingramcontent.com/pod-product-compliance
Lightning Source LLC
Chambersburg PA
CBHW060438130626
46555CB00005B/2416